FOR EMMY

I think one of the saddest and most unfair things about this life is that no matter how vigilant you are, you can't keep loved ones safe. It's not fair, really, because you just can't know how to plan for every danger around every corner. And worse, there are corners that you'd never see, where people can fall right into the pocket of danger. Sometimes those pockets are beyond our grasp.

Originally, I began typing this account in order to blog it to the world. As I've been looking over what I've typed, though, I realized the world doesn't really need to know—probably shouldn't know. My sons, who since each of their births have put the stars in my sky, don't need to know. My husband, with whom I've trusted damn near every little secret in my soul—he doesn't have to know. But truth be told, I can't bear to let the world get swallowed up without writing this down for Emmy. Not that I'm writing anything she didn't know as practically a baby. It's just that as the closest thing to a mother she could remember, it's the only thing I can think to do for her now: type this out and print it before everything goes to hell, then burn it, just like I'd done with everything that has ever bothered me. Write it down and burn it all and let the flames send the bad
feelings up in ash and smoke.

Make it all go away for a time, for both of us...

It's just a symbolic act on my part; I know that. When you're faced with the end of everything, you do what you can to set the world right for a little while. You put old ghosts in their graves, make peace with the past, and set the affairs of your present in order. You occupy your mind by finding ways to distract it. You do those little symbolic things that give you some little feeling of comfort or security or control. It makes things easier, I think, for when you stop fighting fate and close your eyes and hope that when you open them, everything and everyone that matters will find you on the other side.

I could say this isn't about endings or death or fear or even my idea of the other side...but it's really about Emmy, and what happened. So actually, it's about all those things and more.

When my little sister Emmy went missing, she was almost five years old ("four anna half," she'd say, holding up one pudgy little hand of fingers while she tried to figure out how to indicate a half). She was Gerber-baby-pretty: big eyes the color of polished mahogany and soft hair that hadn't quite decided yet whether to be blonde or brown. I used to brush her hair—she wanted to grow it long, like mine—and make little braids for her instead of pigtails, because princesses, she told me, always wore braids. Inevitably, flyaway strands of hair would escape the plaiting to frame her face in wisps.

The day she disappeared, her hair had been in braids like that. She'd been wearing a yellow long-sleeved shirt with little pink and green flowers on it, blue jeans, and her favorite sneakers—Velcro, because she hadn't quite mastered the "bunny ears" technique of tying her shoes yet. I remembered when the police asked me, because I'd picked out her outfit that morning. I'd been picking out her clothes and braiding her hair and making her breakfast and making sure she brushed her teeth and washed her face for years, ever since our mother died.

My father had had a tough time of things, losing his wife, raising two girls, plus juggling long hours at the used bookstore he owned and managed beneath our apartment. Emmy and I always thought he did okay as a dad, but I can see now that even with his sister's occasional and grudging help, it must have taken its toll. I made sure to tell the police when they asked about my father that he handled everything just fine, just like any other man would handle it. And if he felt guilt, helplessness, anger, confusion, I can't see how anyone could blame him. It didn't mean he'd hurt her. No one who looked into that man's eyes could possibly think he would hurt Emmy. I told the police that, too.

I told them how after school, I'd swung by Emmy's preschool and picked her up, then brought her back to my father's store, about three blocks away. When the weather was good, it was a nice walk, and it gave me time to talk to Emmy and hear about what she was learning and what little Tommy Kingsolver did that day during nap time. That afternoon, she was an excited cloud of toddler chatter and meandering stories, and it made me smile to listen to her go on about how Tommy took one of Lila's shoes and how Jennie told Jessica she was a "mean puppethead."

We got to the store at about three o'clock. My dad was going through invoices in his little area behind the counter. Just beginning to gray then, with glasses perched on the end of a strong nose, my father seemed both worn and strong at the same time. His skin was not so much tanned as it was well-worn, the grit of the world worked into the pores and creases. He had strong hands, hands that had lifted us up and swung us around, tucked us in, stroked our hair, hands that had built our playhouses and steadied my bike once the training wheels had come off so that I could find my balance and soar away. There was no anger, no violence in those hands, not ever.

He looked up when we walked in, and his eyes smiled as much as his mouth.

"Well hello there. How are my two lovely ladies this afternoon?"

Excitedly, Emmy launched into Tommy's exploits with Lila's sneaker and the Great Preschool Puppethead War. I laughed, interjecting over-simplified tid-bits about my own day in those grown-up conversations so often held simultaneously over the heads of small chattering children.

I loved them both. Maybe it sounds trite to say we were happy and close, but we were. There were times where Emmy was a tag-along and a pain and a princess who got her way, and there were times my dad was totally uncool, but they were my family, and I loved them.

Sometimes I helped my dad behind the counter, but on slow days, when only the occasional browser wandered in from the over-bright sunshine, I'd roam among the shelves, returning books to their proper places and re-alphabetizing where necessary. It was mindless work I found soothing. Those afternoons spent at the bookstore, inhaling the scent of old paper and old ink, made me feel safe. I felt hugged and held somehow by the solidity of the packed-together books, bricks in a fortress of endless possibility and countless little packaged lifetimes.

Part of the appeal for me—for many book lovers, I imagine—was the age of the books, the idea that these stories had existed in a world before me, blazing trails of novelty and shock, which to me always seemed a kind of artistic bravery and power. My dad had acquired books going all the way back to the pulp-era speculative fiction with covers featuring robots carrying off screaming women and cultists lasciviously groping half-naked virgin sacrifices as they tied them to altars. But he had other books of age and interest, oo—old Civil War diaries, for example. First-edition primers. Early printings of Poe, Asimov, Lovecraft, Faulkner, Mary Shelley, Robert Frost. Dictionaries and Bibles. Ancient tomes claiming secret and forbidden rites and rituals, translated from forgotten languages to Latin.

Sometimes Emmy would tag along with me through the maze, but usually she sat in the Art & Photography section where it met with Political Science and formed a small alcove near the counter. She liked to flip through the pretty pictures in those books. She particularly liked the landscape photography of David Muench and Ansel Adams. Emmy's favorite picture was an Adams print of a winter forest—Yosemite, I think. It was beautiful; the tree looked decorated with tiny crystals all over. I knew that one was her favorite because no matter which book she was flipping through, the large, white Ansel Adams book always lay open to the page with that photo and placed off to the side. I think she was comparing the work of other fine artists and photographers to that one picture, with its perfect clarity, its brilliant and elegant composition. She wouldn't have had the words to explain it, not at four years old, but I think she was looking to find that feeling again, to recapture the thrill of art that moves the soul.

The day Emmy disappeared, I had been wandering from the adventure stories to the speculative fiction books when I noticed the stream of toddler speak had died down completely. The thing about little kids you learn pretty much from the time they figure out how to crawl is that if they're quiet, there's a pretty good chance they're into something they shouldn't be. In a way, this probably follows with people their whole lives, but it's especially true of little kids.

I could hear my father up at the front counter, chatting with a man about baseball books and baseball cards (often, elderly customers struck up pleasant enough conversations with my dad to pass some of their afternoon away). Emmy was quiet. I assumed she had gone to sit and flip through the "pretty pitcher books" but like I said, quiet at least warrants a check to make sure she wasn't "coloring her own pitchers" or anything. I made my way through the Political Science aisle to find her. She wasn't there in Art & Photography, but her little pink backpack was, and so was the large white coffee table book of Ansel Adams opened to the forest in the snow.

I noticed then, although I didn't think much of it at the time, that there was a sour smell clinging to the area where she usually sat—a sharp, metallic kind of tang in the throat. My thought at the time was that it was ozone, but at 16, I'm not sure I would have had the faintest idea what ozone smelled like. It reminded me of thunderstorms, though, and that heavy wet-ground smell.

"Emmy?" I asked the empty space, not quite comprehending her absence. I frowned and turned away, only vaguely aware that the ozone smell was gone before I'd moved completely out of that section.

As I told the police after, I didn't panic just then. Sometimes Emmy sat in the Children's Books section. She liked the toys, and I think she fancied that section her own (if somewhat borrowed) large playroom. She also sometimes sat on one of the reading chairs that occupied a small clearing in the center of the store. At times, she looked through the books on collectible
toys. I didn't panic, as I said, until I had tried each of those places and couldn't find her in any one of them, either.

"Emmy?" I called, not too loud but loud enough to reach her if she were strolling through nearby aisles. "Emmy, where are you?" I checked the back store room, noting the back door, the only other means of entering or leaving the bookstore, was both closed and still locked from the inside. She wouldn't have been able to reach high enough anyway, but it was a relief to see the bolt in place all the same. The bathroom door was open and the light off, but I checked there anyway, then looked around the boxes in case she was playing quietly in a corner somewhere, or had fallen
asleep. She wasn't anywhere in the back room. I came back out into the store area and called for her

again. No one answered.

That, I told the police, was when I got worried. I rushed to the front counter.

"Dad? Dad, where's Emmy? Is she up here with you?"

"Emmy? What? No, she—did you try the Art section?"

I nodded as he came around the counter. The elderly man himself hovered nearby. I'd seen him before in the store, and remembered my father had said his wife, too, had died. He had the kind face of those candy store proprietors in Norman Rockwell paintings, a head full of white hair, wire glasses, and a neat tan coat over a tidy sweater and pants. It's funny, the things people take to themselves as kindnesses to repay; his conversations about books and baseball with my father

helped pass afternoons that were so much emptier after the death of his wife. That bonding, I think— that, and the burgeoning panic on my face— compelled the man to offer his help in looking for Emmy. And he looked in earnest, as if it was his own daughter missing. Funny, the kindnesses

you hold to your heart. That man—Mr. J.B. Ford, Esq. Retired—got at least one free book from my father every time he came into the store after that— mostly books about baseball my father had picked out and set aside for him.

We searched everywhere. We covered the ground again that I had already covered, calling her name. We moved steady and swift through the aisles like a controlled fire, looking over every square inch of the store and turning up nothing, not even a strand

of hair. She couldn't have
gotten out the back door. She couldn't have gotten out
the front door without my dad or Mr. Ford having
seen her. But she wasn't anywhere in the store. So
where had she gone?

I kept going back to the Art & Photography
section, some part of my brain unable to comprehend
the fact that she wasn't sitting there like I'd expected.
Meanwhile, I heard the gravely offered suggestion to
my father to call the police. He did.

My father and I met with a detective named
John Larimar. He walked into the bookstore that day
with power and purpose. I would come to know that
the man nearly always moved and spoke with both
power and purpose. It was a good thing, I think, for a
distraught family to see, when they
felt their most vulnerable and helpless—a man who
would take charge, who would get
things done, who would right this egregious wrong
perpetrated against our little girl by man or
circumstance, and bring her home to us.

"Mr. McCluskey?" the man's voice boomed in
the sickened quiet of the bookstore as he strode from
front door to counter. He wore a dark gray suit a
shade lighter than his hair, a shade darker than his
eyes. He was a boxy man, big, built, square-jawed.
His shoes looked expensive but not new.

"Frank McCluskey? You called about a
missing child." The last was more statement than
question, as if my dad might have forgotten in his
shock why the police were at his door.

"Uh, yes, yes. I'm Frank McCluskey. This is
my older daughter, Dana."

I waved, feeling awkward and out of place among what was sure to be serious grown-up conversation. Teenagers nearly always feel grown up, I think, until police become involved.

The detective nodded at me, then seemed to remember something, paused, and offered me what passed for a warm smile. "Hello Dana, Mr. McCluskey. I'm Detective Larimar. Now, I don't mean to be brusque, but I'd like to ask you a few important questions, and I need you to answer them as honestly and completely as possible. Time is a very critical element here, and I want to make the best use of it that I can to find your daughter."

The speech, however well-practiced it might have been, was effective. I could see just a little of the tension in my father's shoulders let go.

"Sure, sure, detective. Whatever you need."

"Great," Larimar said. He nodded to a slim, dark-haired woman who had unobtrusively brought up the rear, and jerked his pen in my direction. She nodded back and came over to talk to me.

"Hi, Dana," she said, taking out a small notepad and a pen. "I'm Detective Carson. Now I know you're worried about your little sister, and I want you to know we're going to do everything we can to find her, okay?"

I nodded.

"Okay, good. Now, can you go over the events of today for me? Just start at the beginning, and if you can remember anything that seemed different than the usual routine—anyone you don't normally see on your way from school to here, for example—let me know, no matter how small, okay?"

I nodded again, and told her the story I just recounted. I told her every detail I could think of—what Emmy was wearing, what I packed her for lunch, everything she told me about her day. I hadn't noticed anyone strange hanging around, I told her with some distress, and she squeezed my arm and offered me a small smile.

"It's okay, honey. You're doing great. Really. Just tell me about what happened once you got here."

So I told her about the Art & Photography section and the Ansel Adams book, which she asked me to show her. I took her to the alcove of shelves and she took digital pictures of the book, Emmy's little pink backpack, even the shelves themselves. She rifled through the little pink backpack, and took some pictures of its contents. If she noticed the ozone smell, which had faded considerably since I'd first discovered Emmy was missing, she didn't say anything about it.

"Okay," she said with that same small, reassuring smile. "Let's get back to your dad, shall we?"

I nodded, and followed her back to the front counter. My dad looked old, faded somehow. Detective Larimar looked considerably harder than he had when he'd first walked in. At our approach, the questioning seemed to reach an abrupt end, and with a little snap, he flipped his notepad closed. "Mr. McCluskey, we'll be in touch."

I waited until the door had closed on their retreating forms and they were out of view of our front window before running to my dad and hugging him. Feeling him hug me back, the tears came, fast and hard, the sobs muffled by his shirt.

"It's okay, baby," he told me, stroking my hair. "It's okay. They'll find her. They'll find her."

*

They didn't find her. They made several follow-up visits to the store and the house. I think they were looking for evidence that my father hurt her. I got to hate those visits from the cops. My stomach would tie up in knots every time I saw their car pull up across the street or in front of the house. They were supposed to be looking for my sister, trying to figure out how on earth she could have disappeared right out from under us from inside a pretty secure store. Instead, they asked me questions: does your father ever lose his temper? Has your father said or done anything out of the ordinary lately, or right before Emmy's disappearance? Did Emmy seem scared or worried? Did she seem withdrawn lately? Has your father ever hurt you? I didn't like the implications of their questions. My father wasn't like that—he wasn't the kind of man they were suggesting. I mean, my God! Couldn't they see how much he was hurting? How scared he was for his little girl?

That change in people's attitudes toward us went the same way everywhere else, too. At first, the teachers at school were really nice. They gave me free passes for skipping homework, were lenient about me taking make-up tests or retests. I'd always been a good student, and I guess

they wanted to head off any grade-slipping at the pass. My grades did take a bit of a hit but for the most part, I did okay. I didn't have much else to do but study. I was kind of afraid to leave the house, that I'd miss some phone call with news about Emmy or that she'd try to come home, maybe, and no one would be there to let her in. Not that I had a particularly busy social calendar,
anyway. The kids at school were nice enough at first, too—that is, until police frustration influenced the newspapers, and the papers influenced parents, and parents influenced them.

The thing is, part of the discomfort of loss or tragedy is that feeling that something has been done to you, something taken away from you, and that you are alone in that. I don't mean to suggest it is as selfish a feeling as it might sound; it's just that there is something very isolating about loss or tragedy. It puts you on the outside in a very big way, and it's a terrible feeling. You feel marked, somehow. I think that's part of what makes loss so difficult. You're not just assimilating a hollowness into your existence, but reintegrating yourself into the world of people living life again. People can't exist for long on the fringe of life, outside of normal existence. That's my feeling, anyway. People can't tolerate being alone in their misery. I guess that's why there are so many types of support groups. My dad's sister suggested that my dad and I join one. It might have been the most earnestly kind thing to ever come out of that woman's mouth. But my dad was the stoic type, who kept personal things personal and family things inside the family. In his mind, a support group wouldn't reintegrate us with other people, or give us a sense of community; it would frame the picture of loss and fear and differentness that had become our lives, and magnify it. *There are those poor people whose toddler went missing. There's that poor man whose little girl is lost. There's a man to whom* A Missing Child *happened. That man, that sad, sad man, doesn't know, refuses to believe what we all can plainly guess; that man's little girl is dead.*

No, I know my father. He may not have believed in God or vibes in the universe or anything like that, but my dad wouldn't entertain the idea—not out loud, at least—that my little sister was a cold little bundle, alone in the dark and dirt of a ditch somewhere, frightened, mauled, then murdered by the creatures of this world compelled to prey on children.

It seems ironic to type this now, but I think it was easier for my dad to believe she had simply ceased to exist in this world. I'm not sure if that warranted therapy, but it got my father through.

Not that my father was a stubborn man; he would have bent or even broken that self-imposed rule for his girls if we had needed therapy, but I guess I had inherited some of that stoicism from him, too. The school counselor, whom I visited every Wednesday during study hall, seemed like enough for me. She was the one who suggested I write things down, actually. I kept all those old journals in a big shoebox which I never opened until I started this account, but which followed me move to move from apartment to apartment to house. Those jottings helped me write this, all these years later.

And now that I think about it, that school counselor might have given me the idea about burning words. I mean, she gave me a book, if I recall, a self-help book that suggested meditative and symbolic actions to keep a clear, balanced, and peaceful mind. That book suggested the idea that you could write down emotions and feelings – just single words—on scraps of paper, and concentrate on pushing all of that particular feeling from your body and into that scrap of paper. Then you burn it, so no ink part of any letter remained. The idea was that you were purging yourself of the bad feelings, then destroying them, instead of letting them loose into the cosmos to return to you or go to anyone else. Yeah, really new-age surreal stuff, but that one suggestion always struck me as logical, somehow. Obviously, it stuck with me.

Fire makes the bad things go away.

*

Statistics say that approximately 2300 people go missing every day. That's every single day. And most of those are children. In 2001, for example, the federal government counted 840,271 missing persons, and all of those, with the exception of about 50,000, were children. About 100 missing children cases per year are deemed abductions by strangers. Eight out of ten missing children in these cases are female. Although a 1997 study claimed very few missing children are actually found deceased, of the children who are abducted and found murdered, 76.2% are murdered within the first three hours of their abductions.

The thing is, when a child goes missing, you can't possibly know where that child is going to fall in that statistic spectrum. Any missing child is one child too many.

The world is steeped in insensible cruelty, I think. Unanswered questions and nights of worry, fear, and helplessness. Or maybe it isn't cruelty so much as indifference. Maybe the universe doesn't much care if people are in pain, or if people ever get answers. The number of really strange, sad, unexplained missing cases seems to attest to that.

Witness one Lucas Fielder, 18, who left home for his regional Maryland high school on the morning of October 11, 1984. He met up with friends for a smoke before first period. Teachers marked his attendance in homeroom and his first two classes. No one saw him in school after that, or anywhere else, ever again. He was smart, popular, doing well in school. He never took drugs.
He got along with his parents. He was there one minute, and simply gone without a trace the next.

Marguerite Ebbswood, 37, drove through a cool, sunny Ohio morning on November 9, 1986 to pick up her friend Kya Romanova for shopping. They spent a fun afternoon perusing the sales racks and catching up. They were still laughing and talking as they carried their bags back to Marguerite's Ford Escort. She unlocked Kya's door and crossed around to the back of the car, opening the trunk lid. Her sentence cut off mid-word. Kya called out to her, surprised at the sudden silence, and when there was

no answer, she got out of the car to check on Marguerite. She discovered her friend's shopping bag, purse, and keys on the ground by the trunk. There was no
sign of Marguerite anywhere. Searches of the mall grounds turned up nothing.

One June morning in 1990, three-year-old Brice Reynolds was playing out on the front lawn of the Reynolds' Tennessee home when his mother, Carina, happened to look up from her gardening and find him gone. Panicked, she searched the yards, front and back, and up and down the neighborhood streets. Her neighbors grabbed flashlights and helped the police search for four days.
There was no sign of the boy anywhere, other than one of his little shoes, found about six feet to the left of the toys he'd been playing with. Mr. Reynolds was cleared of any suspicion of foul play. His wife, since estranged, currently resides in an assisted living community, not far from the eyes of
sobriety counselors and police alike.

Three separate but eerily similar disappearances happened on June 1, 1994. Portland, Oregon swallowed up Chrissy Schumacher, 33, from the triage waiting area of St. Christopher's Hospital. She had shattered her ankle and couldn't walk. In fact, the pain had made it difficult for
her to focus on much of anything. Her boyfriend had gotten up to get her a glass of water, and when he returned, she was gone. Thinking she had been admitted to see a doctor, he sat patiently to await her return. It wasn't until an attending nurse came out to the waiting area to announce Chrissy was next in line

that her boyfriend realized she was missing. No trace of her was found anywhere in the hospital or on the grounds. Across the country in Manhattan, Jennifer Diaz, 41, vanished from the lobby of Houghlin-McMiller an hour later. She was seen on the surveillance video entering through the revolving doors. On the tape, she slows her pace, looks off screen, then looks around the lobby. Then she continues across the lobby and out of the camera's view. She never made it to her job interview. None of the footage of the surveillance cameras throughout the building show her leaving from any of the exits, nor could it be determined who—or what—had caught her attention. Tatsuo "Craig" Takamura, 55, of San Diego, California, left behind his suit jacket, tie, briefcase, even his wallet in the chair where he'd been waiting for Carol Shields to discuss savings account options with him at Valley National Bank. She'd gone to photocopy his driver's license and some other credentials, as well as pick up extra copies of forms for him to sign, and when she returned to her desk, he was gone. The bank had been fairly busy that morning, and while some of the tellers remembered seeing the distinguished, graying man waiting patiently in the chair, no one could remember seeing him leave.

The list goes on and on. August 29, 2002: Frances and Barney Hillstrom, 76 and 78, respectively, disappeared from their New Mexico home, leaving behind clothes, shoes, purse and wallet—and the family car. February 28, 2003: Pete Lanagan, 26, kissed his date good night and headed back to his car, parked in front of her house. He never made it. The girl's parents found the empty car still parked outside the following morning. On May 14, 2005, Brianna Harvey, 21, of Somerville, Massachusetts texted her boyfriend that she was meeting up with friends at a local pub, O'Sullivan's. She never entered the pub. Her car was found in O'Sullivan's parking lot, keys in the ignition, purse on the passenger seat.

I didn't get too much into the stories about children. Those always set a boulder of fear and disgust rolling around the bottom of my stomach.

What I found most unsettling—still do—about these cases is how surprisingly easy it is to just vanish: to be walking this earth in plain sight of friends and loved ones, and in the space of hours or even minutes, to be gone. For all intents and purposes, to have fallen between the cracks of normal, everyday life. And it's not just rings of standing stones, the Bermuda Triangle, ghost ships, lost highways...it's suburban New Jersey. It's rural Pennsylvania. It's the big city. Where do these people go?

I spent a lot of time thinking about that after Emmy disappeared. My dad was busy...with the store, the police, the search parties, the newspapers. His own thoughts. I don't want to paint the wrong picture here. It wasn't that he didn't care. He was certainly more vigilant of my comings
and goings. He was a lot harder on me for getting to the store late. I don't doubt that a part of him was afraid the outside world would suddenly snatch me away, too. But more often than not, in the security of our too-quiet house, with the doors locked for the

night and the dinner dishes loaded into the dishwasher and a night of mindless TV stretching out ahead of him to keep him company in his insomnia, I lost him. I'd try to watch TV with him, make small talk about our respective days, but

he'd look at me as if he wasn't quite sure who I was, and he'd mumble the kind of nonsense phrases that people say in their sleep. I gave up after a while. In a way, he'd disappear too, into the deep places of his head. And judging from the look on his face during those times, even his expression

when he slept, that interior headscape was some wickedly rough territory. It made me sad that he so often travelled it alone.

Without Emmy to care for and tuck in at night and my father to talk to, I spent a lot of time reading. At first it was formula romance, or the occasional H. Rider Haggard-type adventure. But distractions only work if you can quiet your mind enough to let them take hold. After a while, as the search parties called it quits and the missing posters were covered over and I could imagine my sister's file on Detective Larimar's desk getting shuffled beneath more recent and pressing paperwork, I started to feel helpless and restless. I started looking up facts about missing persons. Statistics. Stories. The libraries around town—there were two—had a surprising number of books on the subject. I wasn't deterred by the low number of recovery stories. I kept looking. I kept searching. I kept the police supplied with information for their records on my sister. I mailed them photocopied leads and any correspondence I received from anyone that might have something to do with my sister. Those were tough, the letters, the notes slid through our mail slot. People in this world are crazy. They're cruel, too.

Some of those correspondences even now make me wonder if the world might not be better off wiped clean of the lot of us.

All those hours spent learning, searching, researching, cross-checking...it didn't do any good, any of it. But I think I knew deep down that it was as much for me as for Emmy. Maybe more for me, if I really get down to the truth of it. It made me feel useful. Active. It gave me a distraction I could let my mind sink into. It kept me sane. I really believe that. It kept me from disappearing into my own head, too.

If you ask any parent if there is a pain worse than the loss of a child, I'm sure the answer would be no. All these years later, with two boys of my own, I understand that. The thought of anything hurting my boys is an ache in every cell, every nerve of my body. As their mother, I want to protect them, keep them safe, warm, healthy, secure, and happy. It tears me up to feel like I failed them in that.

Like I failed Emmy.

But there are worse things than death. There is not knowing. There is wondering every day if that child is scared, confused, wondering why you don't save her, why you don't come, don't you love her anymore? Wondering if she's sick or hungry or missing that teddy bear she never could sleep without. Wondering if someone is hurting her in ways too unspeakable, too stomach-wrenching to even consider. Wondering if wherever she is, she's forgotten about you. Wondering if maybe for her own little sake, death might be better.

If you let thoughts like that get a hold in your mind, it's like asbestos. Your mind tries to bury the unbearable itch of those ideas under layers of denial, forgetting, anger, or grief. Eventually you drown in it, or it rots a big hole in you. And you wonder if maybe for your own sake, death might be better.

Death is an answer, no matter how cold and hard it is. It's irrefutable. It's a fact, and facts put the world solid under your feet again, so you can get your bearings and move forward. Death is a worst-case scenario, but it's an end to the waking death of not knowing. And God help us, we need that. We need to rest in our own peace.

*

Four months later, she came back.

Emmy came right back into our lives, unaccountably, the same way she left them.

With school out, I usually helped my father out for a few hours at the store before going out with friends. That afternoon, I had no other plans but to work at the store, and then go upstairs and read. I hadn't had much of anything else to do of late, as I mentioned. It felt like such a long time since I had done normal things like go to the movies or hang out at the mall with friends, or gossip for hours on the phone about boys. The things the kids in town were whispering about me by then
had gotten more vicious ("See her? Yeah, that's the one. Little sister just disappeared. I think the father

did it. Maybe she helped, even. She always was kind of weird."). By that point, even the last of the kind folks had taken to avoiding us, afraid the pall of unspoken, unofficial tragedy that hung over me and my dad would infect their lives as well, I guess.

Another thing that had slipped into the groove of routine over that summer was checking the Art & Photography section almost obsessively. I checked five, maybe six times an afternoon. It was as if my brain could process the importance but not the fact of my sister's digression from her own routine. I don't doubt there was some deep underlying notion that somehow I'd just missed her, just overlooked some crucial little detail, and if I kept checking, maybe one day I'd find her right where she was supposed to be, safe and sound.

Strangely enough, that's exactly what happened.

It was a late August afternoon, hot and buzzy with the promise of rain so far only hinted at with humidity. I'd been sweeping through the shelves, mindlessly straightening the rows of books. My thoughts, for once, were actually on other things than my sister: the cute guy who smiled at me, for instance, at the local Shell station on my way to the store; what product I could buy for my hair to keep that bit on the left side wavy instead of frizzy; what it might be like to kiss the cute boy from the Shell station. In fact, I could almost feel his green eyes on me, his hands sliding over my hips, or stroking my soon-to-be-nonfrizzy hair.

I nearly tripped over her. My heart jumped in

my chest, that tipsy feeling in my gut that comes with just barely catching one's balance, and I looked down.

In that moment, the bookshelves blurred and bled their color, and nothing else existed inside or outside me except the sight of her, my little sister, my little Emmy, on the floor right in the corner of the Art & Photography section where it meets with Political Science and forms a small alcove
near the counter.

Emmy sat with her little legs stretched out in front of her, wearing the same clothes she'd had on when she disappeared. One hand lay unmoving in her lap. The other lightly tugged one of her braids. Her cheeks were smudged with mud. The same smudges marred the very pale, smooth
baby-skin of her nose, her neck, her hands. It was under her fingernails, too. Her hair looked limp, unwashed, and the braids had taken on the furriness of split ends and strands that had come loose. There was a small scratch on her cheek. Her clothes were stained and faded, but intact. She smelled of ozone – the same smell that had clung to that corner the day she disappeared.

I screamed a kind of choked joy and swooped down to hug her. She was limp, doll-like in my arms. Behind me, I heard my dad's hurried footsteps, and then a kind of choked cry of his own. I let her go, pulling back so he could see her. My tears were warm, washing eyeliner into my eyes and making them burn, but I laughed. I had never felt so good in my whole life.

My dad looked stunned. He sank to his knees,

scooping her up gently and holding her tight. He looked as if the breath he'd been holding in his chest, the one that had grown stale, hard, and painful, had suddenly been let go. He also looked scared, almost child-like. I think he thought he could make some wrong move, say the wrong word, and she'd crumble in his arms or maybe pop like a bubble and just be gone again.

"Emmy," he asked breathlessly, tears glittering in his eyes. "Baby, oh baby...where were you?"

*

We found out quickly enough that she couldn't tell us where she was. I don't think that was just because of her limited toddler vocabulary. I don't know if any adult could have explained it better. She didn't seem to be hurt physically, not that we could see from first glance, but just...off. Distracted. Confused.

Almost all of Emmy seemed to be there—almost. That realness, that thereness that characterizes people we know and love, was missing. That same thereness was missing from her eyes, too. It was like all the things that make children loveable, like their laugh, the wonder and excitement and the honest and unconditional love—all that was just...gone. Whatever she had been through, whatever she had seen and wherever she had been, it changed her.

The doctors examined her. The dazed blankness in her eyes they attributed to shock and a slight case of malnutrition; otherwise, they said, she was okay. No signs of assault, sexual or otherwise, no injuries—well, except for a bite on her left hand that had begun to heal. There was no sense swabbing it and the healing process had tugged it grossly out of shape somehow, so they couldn't determine for sure what had caused the bite, but they ran blood tests and counts and checked charts and graphs and she was found to be in good physical health, at least.

The state of her mental health, though, seemed to completely baffle them. She responded to her name, to simple questions or commands. She recognized basic things – colors and shapes, animals, places like school and the store. She recognized our dad and me, and pictures of uniformed people like firemen and policemen. But her sense of time was way off. She didn't much understand the concept of the past or the future. She mixed up days. And physical contact of any kind, except what she initiated herself, was met with violent shaking.

God, baby, I used to think, looking at her playing with joyless silence in a corner with her toys, the light and laughter gone out of her. *Where were you? And who hurt you, wherever you where?*

She'd missed the last two and a half months of preschool, and the doctors suggested that at that young age, she should take a year to rest, to adjust to being home. They thought in time, the trauma would work itself to the surface or work itself out completely. She is young, they told us. Children are amazingly resilient. I know they suspected something had happened, that maybe she'd seen something or been through something horrible enough to dry up her speech to drips and drabs, but try as they might, no one could seem to get whatever it was out of her. The police talked to her, child psychologists talked to her, but no carefully worded question could elicit any answers whatsoever. My father even got her a child therapist, whom she met with once a week.

"So, Emmy, I see you like to color," the child therapist asked her one session. It was early on in the therapy; Emmy had insisted in her mostly non-verbal way that I stay with them, and the therapist acquiesced.

Emmy didn't answer. She kept coloring inside a brown rectangle, a lot of different-colored squares and lines.

"Emmy, what are you drawing?"

"Books," her little voice answered from beneath the curtain of blonde hair. She wouldn't let me braid it anymore. She barely let me brush it those days without screaming bloody murder when I touched her.

"Books, huh? What kind of books?" The therapist leaned in, not so close as to be invasive, but close enough, I thought, for conspiratorial conversation.

"Art books," came the little voice again.

"Can you tell me what's in the art books, sweetie?"

She didn't answer.

The therapist, a tidy woman of forty with a smart cut of dark hair, shared a reassuring look over her head.

"If I gave you a clean piece of paper, do you think you could draw something from the place you were when you weren't with Daddy and Dana?"

Emmy didn't answer that, either, at least not with words. Her crayon strokes, though, were getting harder, and the color spread on the paper was taking on a waxy intensity.

"Emmy, why don't you tell me about Daddy's bookstore?"

The little curtain of hair swung back and forth with the effort of hard-coloring the books. Emmy seemed to think about the therapist's question as she wore down the point of a red crayon. Finally, she said, "It has a hole."

This time, the therapist's look was less comforting.

"A hole, sweetie? What kind of hole?"

Emmy's crayon moved faster.

"Can you tell me about the hole, Emmy?"

The crayon started going out of her self-imposed book lines. If her coloring was any indication of her mental state, she was running outside her own lines in her head.

"Emmy, where is the hole in Daddy's bookstore?"

The picture under Emmy's hand was no longer a bookshelf full of art books, but a massacre scene, with red running all over everything.

"Emmy—"

The crayon broke in half in her hand. "No!" she shouted, finally looking up. For a second—just a second—it looked like her face blurred. Actually, no, it wasn't blurring so much as morphing. For just that second, the anger in her face was personified, and the features looking up from the shunted-aside blonde bangs were not Emmy's, nor anything resembling human at all.

I was sure from the look on her face that the therapist saw the change in Emmy, too. Still, she pressed with a suggestion. "Emmy, if someone took you, maybe someone who got in or out through the hole...we can close it up. We can make sure we catch whoever took you so that you never have to worry again."

Emmy shook her head violently.

"We can make the nightmares stop—"

Emmy started to scream. It took a long time for the therapist to calm her down.

After, the therapist and I exchanged a few words while Emmy lay on the waiting room couch, exhausted from her tantrum.

She told me she had to push a little harder this time, because what Emmy said could potentially catch the person who took her (if she had indeed been taken) or explain where she had gone.

Emmy never told her, though. The therapist didn't have the right words to unlock the door behind which Emmy kept everything deeply hidden in her mind. And Emmy had neither the means nor desire to let anyone in on that secret.

So far as anyone could tell, she simply ceased to exist for four months.

*

I know I said knowing is better than not knowing, and I think in most cases where people go missing, that holds true.

But when your missing loved one comes

back... Well, I just think that sometimes, knowing is worse. Like when the knowledge is about something you can't change.

Given a choice and some time to think it through, I can't imagine many people would choose to know the hour of their own deaths. Likewise, given the choice and some time to think it through, I doubt anyone would want to know the hour of mankind's extinction. In either case, we're comfortable with a vague and distant future date. When the choice is taken away, though, it's the knowing that plunges us back into that waking death, that waiting for the inevitable end. So, do you sit and wait for it? Try to stop it? Go with the hope that death is better? What do you do then?

But I'm getting way ahead of myself. I think I've done a pretty good job so far of writing down a coherent account, and it wouldn't do Emmy or me any good to wax on a philosophical tangent now.

I mentioned pockets at the beginning of this, because I think it best explains where Emmy really did go. The fabric of reality has pockets—little off-shoots connected but separate from it, places existing outside the world we know. The thing is, pockets are rarely empty. And I know that these pockets are no exception.

I got an idea of where Emmy really was during those four months because of a few incidents which occurred in those few months after her return.

The first, I guess, was her mention to the therapist of the hole in my dad's used bookstore and the follow-up to that revelation. The therapist had relayed the events of the session to my father as well, explaining that it was possible that there was another means of ingress or egress in the store, or at the very least, something that suggested it might be, at least to Emmy. She said it might go miles in terms of reassuring Emmy if the hole could be discovered and sealed up in front of her. She had no idea, at the time, how crucial a suggestion that was, but then, at that time, we had no idea, either. We just took Emmy to stay with my aunt, who curtly reminded us to pick her up before her bedtime, and then headed back to the store to try to locate the "hole" Emmy was referring to. But where the hell could there be a hole that my father and I wouldn't have seen?

The store was closed for the evening. My father and I stood by the front counter, staring at the expanse of the store. The whole store was only one floor, about 1300 square feet, including the store room. The building used to be a warehouse, and above steel beams, the metal roof looked to us to be intact. The shelves, mostly a dark, sturdy wood, stood flush with the walls, a careful arrangement that left no unused space. The store room comprised a small bathroom with toilet, sink, and mirror, and the back door, locked. Back there, we had stacks of boxes and towers of books, as well as a small folding table where my father kept the coffee machine and a few mugs. It was possible, we supposed, that there might be a "hole" of some sort among the stacks where someone could have hidden, maybe, but...

We exchanged looks.

"What do you think we're looking for?" I asked my dad.

He shrugged, a baffled, unshaven man in an

old shirt. Even then, I think I knew what he was feeling. That's one of the surreal aspects of the teenage years, those occasional glimpses of adult life, those flashes of understanding. And I knew—I understood—that my dad felt helpless. He felt like he was being given a chance to help heal his little girl from whatever had been done to hurt her, and he had no clue how to complete the task. It's been my experience in the years since that few things render a man's self-esteem so low as not knowing how to act, especially when action is necessary to protect a loved one, or soothe a hurt.

"Why don't we...just start at one end and check it all?"

He nodded, relief bringing color back to his face. We moved together, checking every square inch of open space and all the walls that surrounded it for something, anything, that could be construed as a hole. We found nothing—not even a drainage grate. Nothing she could see as a hole.

We were working up a sweat moving boxes around in the back room when I finally said, "This is ridiculous."

"What?" My dad huffed and put down the box he was lifting.

I sighed. "There's no hole here, Dad. There's nothing. Emmy...she just...I don't think she..." And maybe it was exhaustion or fear or relief. Maybe it was frustration. I just broke down. My father navigated around the boxes and put an arm around my heaving shoulders. I cried into his old shirt. My father didn't say anything. He just let me cry. There wasn't anything to say. We both knew the facts, and those facts made no sense. There was no hole in the store. There was no way Emmy or anyone else could have gotten in or out of that store without one of us seeing her leave. So where had she gone?

The second thing happened in October. I had come to find the walk to the store from school a good time to think, and in early October, it was just warm enough to still be enjoyable. The leaves spread their brilliant wildfire above our heads, little licks of which had begun to drop to the street as well.

Luckily, Emmy's old pre-school was a detour on the way to the store, and one that I could now avoid. I had followed the familiar route the first few times and it hurt to see those little kids—little girls like Emmy, with flyaway braids and Velcro-flaps on their shoes instead of ties, and little flowered shirts and dresses. It hurt to see whole playgrounds full of children that were safe, whose whereabouts were known. Children who got to go home every day and tell their parents about their day and get tucked in and read a bedtime story. I stopped walking that way early on, and I was glad that, even with Emmy back safe, I could avoid walking past it still. I had a feeling that it would still hurt to see those children. To see bright eyes and hear laughter, to see animation in the little faces and bodies. Children who were plain and open and untouched, who didn't scream when you touched them or stand in the middle of the bedroom and stare at the wall, humming the same repetitive five or six notes while tears rolled down their once-chubby little cheeks.

I found my dad reading a magazine at the front counter when I arrived at the store. He looked up and smiled at me when I walked in, but it was a tired smile. It had come to replace his real one, and although it was genuine, it was only a shade of what had come before it.

"Where's Emmy?" I leaned over the counter and put by backpack by his keys.

"She's over in the Children's section." There was a pause. "She's quiet today." That was how my father explained those moods where Emmy least seemed like the little girl we knew, when something in her voice and her eyes changed. It was when she seemed the farthest away from us—
farther, even, than when she had actually been gone.

I nodded, disappointed, and headed back to the Children's section.

I found her coloring, a pad of paper on her lap and crayons everywhere, rolling into the crevices of the big easy chair on which she sat.

"Hi, baby," I said, crouching beside the chair. "Whatcha drawing?"

She didn't answer. I didn't expect her to. I looked over her shoulder at the paper, and immediately, my stomach wrenched itself into a knot.

Two grayish orbs hung in a sky she had topped off in black. I assumed those were moons. On the ground, there were two figures. The smaller one had strokes of blonde hair, and wore a yellow shirt and blue jeans. The upside-down "u" of her mouth and the strokes of red on one arm bothered me. So did the larger figure, which wasn't a stick-figure representation of a person at all. It had a bulbous black trunk inside which Emmy had drawn a maw stretched wide, lined with irregular red triangles I assumed were teeth. Snaking from the trunk were lots of arms and legs from which Emmy had drawn long hairs or spikes. In one of the twisting arms was another stick-figure girl with black hair, the mouth a lopsided "o." Red strokes from the stick-figure girl rained down over the swollen body of the black beast. On the ground around the little blonde Emmy figure were other odd shapes with legs and tails, ostensibly some kinds of animals, and they, too, had been scribbled and crisscrossed with waxy red carnage. Something like a tree, although it had streaks of blue and orange, clawed the sky, leafless and sinister. To the right of the tree, just over the horizon, Emmy had drawn a large eye. Although this was in the background, she had given it the most attention, alternating between yellow and orange with slow, deliberate strokes.

It was a four-year-old's rendering, crude and perhaps oversimplified, but those almost incidental elements gave me the distinct impression that she was drawing something she had seen rather than made up. Something she no doubt dreamed every night.

As soon as she lost interest in coloring it and strolled off toward the shelves of children's books, I rolled it up and carried it up to my backpack. I brought it with us to therapy that night, and after their session, I showed it to the therapist while she was occupied with toys.

The therapist unrolled it on her desk and studied it for several moments before making a clicking sound with her teeth.

"What do you think it is?" I couldn't keep my voice from sounding anxious.

"I think I'd have to try to get her to tell me about it. It could be one of her nightmares, or an extrapolation of one of her fears. The gore does seem to indicate that she was witness to—possibly even involved in—a certain level of violence. But she's obviously substituting."

I guess my expression must have given away my confusion, because she added, "The monster, here, with all these tentacles. The monster who seems only to be a mouth and arms. I think this is her way of describing whoever she was with for four months. Perhaps he or she was loud or talkative, maybe shouted at her a lot. The mouth. And the number of tentacles here suggests an inescapable grasp. This person is all mouth and hands, and those hands suggest violence."

"No," Emmy said behind us, and we both jumped. Her voice held that strangely adult and alien quality that more and more replaced the softness of her own little voice.

"Emmy—"

"It's not a person."

"Okay." The therapist's voice was placating, comforting. I don't think she liked that new voice either, or the subtle threat its roughness seemed continually to imply. "What it is then, sweetie?"

I saw the change in her face for just a second, just a tightening and stretching of the jaw, a darkening of the eyes, and swimming up in them, a foreign and malign intelligence. It was there just for a second, but I know I saw it. I'd swear to God I saw it.

Then she bowed her head, clutching one of the dolls the therapist let her play with after sessions. She little grip tightened around the body of the doll, and she started to mewl. That mewling melded into a whine which rose both in pitch and volume, a siren, a wail of pain and fear. She shook the doll violently, and the effort rippled the wail, as if the doll were screaming.

The wail broke off suddenly, as did the shaking, and she dropped the doll. When she looked up, it was her face, her eyes gazing at us, wide and confused and scared. She took in what could only have been astonishment on our faces and that seemed to fuel the fear. She looked down at the picture on the therapist's desk and muttered something neither of us caught.

"Emmy?" I took a step toward her, put a tentative hand on her shoulder. She didn't move or scream or pull free, but she did look up at me.

"It's the demon," she said, and started to cry. It was the last any of us could get her to say on the subject.

The third thing happened during inventory day, the last Sunday of the month of November. We closed down the store, and my dad and I each took a section of the store to go through, pouring through the titles on the shelves and checking them off on a triplicated checklist. Emmy was sent behind the counter. Since her return, my father wasn't comfortable with her wandering the shelves anymore.

I had just finished the Occult and Magic section and was about to start on the History and Military sections when I heard a noise from a familiar corner of the store, a corner unused by Emmy since April. I paused, backtracking to the Political Science shelf that faced out toward the rest of the store.

From over the shelf, I heard the sounds of movement, and a low rumble which reminded me of the sound a hungry stomach makes.

"Emmy?"

There was no answer from her, but I felt a little tugging at the hem of my shirt. I looked down. She stood there, her eyes wide, the first intense emotion I'd seen in months making them shine. She looked terrified.

From over the shelf came the rumble again, and a wet plopping sound.

I took no more than a step or two in the direction of the sound when I felt her tugging harder. "No, no, Dana," she whimpered, that shine of fear glittering now with tears as well. "Nonono."

"Baby, I'm just going to go see—"

"No!" she grabbed my arm, and her grip held surprisingly strong.

"Emmy, if it's an animal or something that got stuck, I have to see." I tried to gently pry her fingers from my arm, but her grip tightened to a painful vise-like hold. Beyond us was a faint, far-away wail, a sound coming from the end of a long tunnel, a sound over a bad phone connection. There was a sucking sound followed by a wet sliding, and a thwap against the books that wiggled the shelf between us and whatever it was.

"It's bad," Emmy whispered. "It's bad. It's bad."

"Em, it's okay, it's just—" A sudden thought occurred to me about holes and hand-bites. Her eyes were on the bookshelf that obscured the animal, if it was one, from our view. I took her chin gently and guided her face toward me so I could look her in the eye. "Do you know what it is over there?"

"They bite," she whispered, and her gaze flitted back to the shelf.

"What bites?" My own voice barely cracked a whisper.

"The demons..." The tears left shiny little tracks on her doll cheeks. I felt sweat bead up on my neck and under my arms.

"Emmy, go get Dad."

She tore her gaze away from the shelf and looked at me. I let go of her chin.

"Go. Get him right now. Tell him I said it's an emergency."

She nodded slowly, and walked off. Sometimes she seemed to understand simple commands, but couldn't seem to carry them all the way out. I hoped to God this wasn't one of those times. It slapped the shelf again, and this time, the shelf threatened to topple a few books onto the floor. Whatever it was did not sound like something I wanted to face myself. I was sure, though, that it had something to do with Emmy's disappearance, and where she might have been while she was gone.

I crept slowly around the Political Science shelf, following the wet, slithery sounds. I heard it wail again, the sound fading in and out, as if it somehow straddled here in the bookstore, and there...there, wherever Emmy had been for four months.

When I rounded the corner and stood facing the alcove that the Art & Photography section formed by the counter, all the air rushed out of my lungs, along with the strength in my legs. I sank where I stood.

The thing making the wet slapping and slithering sound was long and black, tapering to a coarse point at one end. Long spiny needles, some the length of my forearm, ran irregular rows all over it. It glistened with its own kind of moisture, which was drying on the thinner end and causing the black to crack like dry rubber. The cracks looked painfully raw, with sub-cracks spider-webbing along the rough edges. A kind of dark purple jelly oozed from where the cracks ran deepest.

Wherever it paused, a kind of mucus, thick and clotted, pooled beneath it, and between the thrashing and snapping, it seemed to be trying to rub the rawest parts in the mucus. It stank, too—the heavy, wet ozone smell I was coming to recognize and something else. A sickness smell that reminded me, again inexplicably, of something I would not, at 16, have any real experience with. It was a rot-smell, a gangrene and leprosy smell—decay before death.

Following the length of the thing to what should have been its source, I expected some bulk that drove it. There was nothing. I tried peering behind the root of it, but more of it vanished behind a corner or boundary that I somehow couldn't see. I leaned slowly in the other direction.

What I saw looking at it head-on reminded me very much of heat waves: that blurry colorlessness that wavers the rest of the world if you look right through it. It was gathered into a clearly delineated square about three feet across by four feet high. The rest of the body connected to the tentacle thing seemed to be submerged in this wavery patch and beyond view. Through the patch, I could see the art books, skewed, on the shelf behind it.

Heavy air seeped back into my lungs, air saturated with the ozone-smell and that throat-coating odor of decay. And that's when I screamed.

My observation of the thing maybe ran the span of about three minutes. The events after my scream were possibly the incidents of a few minutes more. It's funny how time seems to bend and stop or loop around itself, when you're absolutely terrified.

The whip of the tentacle stopped mid-air, and suddenly five or six eyes opened up in the black among the tines. All of them ocused immediately and intensely on me. What had been a hurried walk became a rush of footsteps as my father came running. The tentacle shot out and wrapped around my right arm. By sheer luck, my flesh fell between the spines instead of being impaled on one of them, but the sensation was no less awful. Nothing I had ever felt or have felt since made my skin crawl in such utter disgust as touching that black, glistening flesh, both rubbery and hard, the mucus burning a terrible rash across the skin of my bicep.

Then, the tentacle tugged. I fell forward, and the carpet beneath me slid away. The length of the thing was shorter now, and I saw why. It was retreating back into the wavery patch—and it was dragging me with it!

I felt another grip on my other arm, and the backwards jerk of force. "I gotcha, baby. I gotcha. Don't worry." It was my father. He shifted his grip.

Again the tentacle yanked me forward, and again my father responded with force in the opposite direction.

"Daddy!" I screamed. "Don't let it take me! Please God, don't let it take me!"

"I won't, baby. I've got you." His voice was calm but strained. His arms slipped around my waist, and he dropped a fist over my shoulder to pound between the long spikes. One of those spikes angled and dug into my shoulder, and an unbearable burning pain shot down the arm. The
fleeting thought of poison crossed my mind, but it was flushed out by the fear of losing my arm. The tentacle tightened, and the pressure made me scream again.

In kind, it bellowed from beyond the wavery patch.

My father gave one more swift yank and for just a moment, the bulk behind the tentacle was caught in the momentum. A gust of fetid smell blew outward, and with it, the bulk itself came into view. It was that same lightless black but devoid of spikes. Instead, a split in the flesh yawned open roundly, and rows and rows of teeth spiraled downward into the darkness of its throat. From that tooth-lined split came another bellow, and this time, here in our world, it was loud enough to shake the shelves around it.

It yanked hard, pulling the mouth-bulk out of sight again, and I nearly slid out of my father's grasp. I screamed again, sure that this thing would pull my arm off, or worse, would pull me clean out of this world and into whatever kind of hellish space could spawn tentacled things like that.

"Daddy!" I screamed one last time.

There was a sudden grinding noise then, like metal scraping metal, and the thing roared from the other side. The wavery patch vibrated violently, splashed outward, then vanished completely. Whatever had opened suddenly closed, sealing off the roar and the mouthy bulk and whatever else lay on the other side. The pressure in my arm abruptly let off, and the tentacle fell to the ground. I went tumbling backward into my dad.

For a long time, we sat where we were, sprawled on the floor in the Art & Photography section, staring at the amputated tentacle on the floor. Without sustenance from the bulk it belonged to, it dried of mucus quickly, cracking and then fully splitting open. The smells that had accompanied its thrashing had faded as the internal jelly of it dried to a crust. It crumbled into pieces on the floor, and those pieces disintegrated to powder. After a few moments, even the powder had somehow broken down to nothing.

The skin of my face felt tight with the tears that had dried on it. I couldn't speak. My father and I just stared at the space where it had been.

Behind us, Emmy laughed, and the cold humorless tone of it sounded as alien and terrifying as the tentacle thing.

*

"What was it, Dad?"

It was about 8:30 in the evening, and Emmy had gone to bed. It would be another long night of fitful half-sleep, punctuated by nightmares for her.

We had the baby monitor (it seemed we had just finally put it away in the closet not too long ago) with us in the store so we could hear her right away if she needed us upstairs, and judging by the ragged breathing, she was mostly asleep. At least she hadn't begun to whimper yet, and so for the next few hours, her exhaustion would give my father and I time to talk and to figure out a plan.

"I don't know, honey. I..." His gaze trailed to the shelves surrounding the place where the tentacle had been. It was quiet over there now—no growling or wailing—but that ozone smell still hung in the air, diffused as it spread through the bookstore. It was a reminder that we hadn't imagined it, that it had really happened. I looked at my arm, and the assorted bruises that covered it, wrist to shoulder. Another reminder. Larimar would have a field day with those on his next visit, maybe think my dad had finally cracked and was trying to break my arm. Bastard. I shrugged on the sweat jacket I had brought, more because I didn't want to look at the bruises than because I was cold. Still, I shivered inside it.

"What if it comes back?"

"It won't," he said.

"What if it does?"

"We'll make sure it doesn't." He looked at me solemnly. "We'll close it up."

"Close it?"

"The hole. The bleary space that...that thing came through. The rift. I mean, that's got to be what it is, right? Some kind of rift in space. Some kind of anomaly. There's no other explanation for—" He stopped abruptly. "There's got to be a way to close it up."

"How?"

A long silence followed, finally broken when my father said, "There are spells. There have got to be spells. Witchcraft, occult studies, demonology—some study must have a means of sealing up whatever keeps tearing open in my bookstore."

"I...I don't...I can't..."

My father said, "Dana, there is something very, very wrong here, and it defies every experience and every belief about this universe I've carried with me my whole life. I never believed in ghosts or ESP or alien visitations or anything of the sort. I don't know how to explain what happened this afternoon, only that my senses confirm that it did happen. That's all I have to go on. We both saw that thing. Smelled it. Heard it. Felt it." He scratched at the unshaven scruff on his chin. "I'm no scientist, but I'm pretty sure whatever nearly pulled your arm off is not from this world. So nothing from this world is going to protect us from it."

He was right. Although he hadn't said it, the experience afforded sensory proof and then some; it wasn't just seeing it in the rubbery flesh, or smelling it; it charged the air around it with its alienness; every cell, every fiber of our being in contact with or proximity to the thing screamed to us that it didn't belong here.

There was more to it—more than I ever said to him or anyone, because at the time I was too scared to fully take it in and later, it seemed dangerous somehow to say it all out loud. But if I'm going to purge all the bad, every crazy, awful element to this, I might as well admit it here. I won't go so far as to say it talked to me, because it wasn't words, not even thoughts. When it touched me, though, I could sense its own confusion, its anger, its pain from exposure to our atmosphere. Beneath that was a pool of latent but constant feelings, and I could feel a sentient hate, a powerful

hunger to move, to rend, to continue on, to pull apart. I don't know if it knew any more about our world than we had known about theirs; I don't know if it knew its tentacle was drying up in another dimension, but I'm sure—I could feel it—that it knew of rifts in vague terms: doorway, food, outside. It knew enough about rifts to see them as places to fish for food, but not to cross. Crossing, it felt, was for others.

Crossing was for others.

There were other things in that world—things four-year-olds saw and drew as eyes, maybe—that could cross through just fine and survive. Maybe go hunting. Emmy, after all, had survived that atmosphere over there. If these rifts grew big enough at some point...

"...should have something we can use," my father was saying, and I shook my head, pulled from my thoughts.

"What?"

"I said, I acquired a book years ago—at a garage sale, of all places. You never know where you'll find a good...anyway, this book. After flipping through it, I decided not to put it out for sale.

Sometimes you just get a feeling about things, you know?"

I nodded. Oh, I knew, all right.

"It wasn't anything so esoteric and coincidental as believing it had powerful spells in it, although I suppose it does, to the people who believe that sort of thing. No, see, the reason I didn't put it up for sale was because of an old photograph I found tucked into the back of the book." He scratched absently at his chin again, and this time, tiny droplets of blood dotted the whiskers where he'd scratched himself. "It was a photograph of a woman who looked just like your mother."

I said nothing. My dad almost never talked about my mom (I think a part of him needed to believe she'd also simply ceased to exist in this world, in order for him to survive her death).

"Beautiful woman, she was." I didn't know if he was talking about the woman in the picture, or my mother, but I supposed it didn't matter. "In the picture, the woman is standing on a porch, and behind her is a lake. There are sailboats way in the background. The woman has on a pretty sundress. She looks sad."

"Dad, I don't—"

His weary expression was what stilled the sentence still in my mouth.

"There was an inscription on the back: *'To Lila—I would have given you the world, or given the world to preserve you. –K'* And I got it in my head that this sad woman was lost to K, whoever he was. And judging by the book's contents, it made me wonder just what this man had been willing to sacrifice to 'preserve' her. It somehow didn't seem right to me then to sell off the sum total of a man's efforts to protect his woman." His chuckle was dry and humorless.

"Probably sounds silly. Sentimental. But it was right after your mom died, and the sad woman—Lila, I guess—looked so much like her, and..."

I touched his hand, and he came back to the here and now. "Where's the book now?"

"In the store room." He walked around the counter.

"And you think it will help?"

A pause. He turned. "Stay here. Keep an ear on her," he added, nodding at the baby monitor.

From the monitor, Emmy slept the sleep of the dead.

*

My father had always been a planner. He didn't like surprises, he always said, and if there was a job to do, he believed the time it took to be prepared was well worth the investment. His first foray into the occult was no exception.

We didn't speak about the book for the rest of the week. I watched him read it, his thin black reading glasses perched on his nose and a notebook and pencil on the side table next to his chair. Occasionally, he'd jot something down in the notebook. I had questions, but the look on his face deterred me from asking. Early on one night after dinner, I was alone in the living room, and the book was on the side table by his chair. I lifted the cover.

"Dana."

I jumped. My father hardly ever raised his voice.

He stood in the shadows between the kitchen and the living room, and for a moment, he looked to me like a stranger.

"You don't need to know what's in that book, honey," he said in a softer tone. "You just need to trust me."

*

The last favor my father ever asked of his sister was to watch Emmy overnight the following Friday.

We had to wait for the rift to open again. It could have been months or even years—a part of me hoped it would take so long. But it didn't. The following Friday, my dad noted the ozone smell, the smoky distortion of the air. He made me take Emmy upstairs right away and wouldn't let us into the store the rest of the day. I wanted to believe time had healed the rift and it had scarred over. It hadn't, and my father acknowledged this with a grim satisfaction. He was a man of action, and he wanted things put right, but he needed to know that he wouldn't be doing more harm than good. He needed proof that the only option was to dabble in things people ought not to dabble in. My father didn't like surprises.

He got the confirmation he needed: the thick smell, damp ground and strange air, wailing and atavistic growling. The rift was open again.

That Friday night, my father made us a nice dinner, and as we ate, he told us stories, laughing and joking with us like he had before Emmy disappeared. I laughed with him. We needed it, all three of us— one night of normalcy, I think, especially that night. Even Emmy seemed to come back to us for a bit, smiling and giggling. It had been so, so long since we'd heard her laugh...

After dinner, my father sent me up to pack her little overnight bag while he took care of the dishes. We brought her over to my aunt's, and when my father hugged her, there was a kind of finality in it, a kind of desperation, as if he could soak up enough of her essence in that hug to carry with him always. It was the kind of hug, I thought then, that you'd give someone if you knew it would be the last time. If you knew you might go missing.

I hugged Emmy good-bye, too, and then she went wordlessly into the spare bedroom my aunt had made up for her. She didn't like my aunt, having that child's sense of adults who are intensely uncomfortable around children. My aunt said little to her, either, or to us. She was a small, sharp woman, like a piece of curled metal with edges that bit if you handled them wrong. She was normally nosy, but something in the way my father looked, in the tone of his eyes and his voice, kept her from asking questions that night. He had that quality, lately, that ability to convey to others that they should keep their distance and keep their mouths shut. I guess Emmy wasn't the only one who had picked up something alien.

When we got to the store, it was dark, a cold night feathered with frost. My father locked the door behind me and we made our way in the dark to the front counter. He turned on one lamp. He had several things laid out on the counter—a white candle, a blue candle, a cloth pouch, a lighter, some chalk, and a salt shaker. He gathered them up silently and I followed him as he carried them to the Art & Photography section.

We crouched on the floor. This was the closest we had ever been to the rift, and up close, it moved the air somehow in a way that made me nauseous and hurt my head. I wasn't touching it but I could feel it, going against my own personal grain. I'm not sure how to put it, but that seems as close to the feeling as I can get. It went against the flow of this world, in a way that rubbed the systems of the body the wrong way.

My dad swallowed loudly, scratching at his chin. He lit the blue candle first, and then opened the cloth pouch. There was a black powder inside which he sprinkled in strange shapes and lit on fire. It sparked and I jumped. He told me to light the white candle.

"Dana." The sharp voice again. It made me jump, but I took the lighter and lit the candle.

The rift wavered. Something just beyond the opening growled. He threw powder at the blurry spot and said more words, and for a moment, I thought I saw through to the other side—just a glimpse, just a piece of darkening purple sky, a bruised and angry sky with storms that could tear through our world, and...God, I still remember...the eye. The eye...

My father drew frenzied symbols with chalk, tossing salt as he chanted. His words picked up speed, and my breath caught with the urgency in his voice.

I don't know the words my father used, and honestly, I don't think I want to know. I think some things probably shouldn't be repeated. Maybe it sounds superstitious, but I'm glad I don't know them because I don't know what would happen if I wrote them here. If I read them back to myself, even in my head.

What I do know is that those words weren't in any language I had ever heard before or since, and my father, who had clearly studied the words, maybe even practiced them until that hard, inarguable foreign quality took up residence in his eyes, never repeated them or told me what they meant.

"Touch the chalk," he commanded sharply, nudging me forward. I placed my hands on the symbols nearest to me. He dove back into marking the floor with them, the chalk splintering from the pressure of his drawing. From the rift, clear strands of something not quite liquid or solid shot out and sprayed my cheek. I whimpered. I could barely suck in a breath to cry. The words my father wove into a breathless chant felt dirty on me, over me, around me. I got the feeling again that I was crouched near a stranger.

His chant rose in volume, the same six or seven words over and over, louder and louder, and suddenly the wavery part yawned open, and there was the eye, right there, looking at me! Looking through me! Looking into the deepest parts of me and studying me so that no matter where I went, there would be a rift, and from that rift, knowing my print on the world, it would find me, it would see me, and it would tear open everything about me to dry and crack and die in its world, and—

—I screamed and screamed, loud but not louder than my dad's words, or the crackle of fire as he tossed the powder at the eye and lit it all on fire....

The wail from that eye, from behind that eye, shook the shelves so hard that books fell, their hard corners finding the soft parts of me. The fire blazed up and my dad cried out as the flame enveloped his hand. There was a flash of painful brightness, and then everything—the eye, the distortion of air, that terrible angry storm-filled sky, and most importantly, the damp, metallic ozone smell—it all winked out. Like Emmy, it was there one minute, and then simply gone.

My father flopped back, cradling his burnt hand in his t-shirt. With his good hand, he pulled me close and hugged me so tightly it pushed air from my chest. "You okay, baby? You okay?"

"Is that it?" I asked, panting heavily.

I looked at my dad. There were tears in his eyes, but it was my dad, inside and out.

That hardness was gone from him.

"Baby," he said, smiling softly, "isn't that enough?"

*

I'd give anything to be able to write something about a happy ending here. Would it sound corny to cap off a story like this with a happily ever after? Hell, if I could say it all worked out, I wouldn't give a hot damn how it sounded. I could spin a nice little ending about how I grew up and got married to my soul mate, had two beautiful boys, moved to a pretty little suburb up by the Delaware Water Gap. I could say we sealed up that rift between dimensions, and my dad lived out a quiet life amidst the shelves of books he so very much loved, in the store he could once again see as a haven and not a portal to unimaginable horror. I could describe how Emmy grew up pretty and strong and that the nightmares eventually faded, and she went off to college and met a boy who worshipped the ground she walked on. I could tell how in sealing up that rift behind the bookcase, we forced all the bad, strange air from that other place out of her lungs, those pictures out of her head, and that haunted look out of her eyes, and we sent it all back to where it came from and closed off its access to this world forever.

I could say all those things, but it didn't happen quite that way. Scars happen. Just because you survive, that doesn't mean you go on truly living. It's not like the movies. People don't just face down demons, then clean the blood off their faces, change their clothes and go take a nap. You don't sweep up the remaining clutter of the whirlwind battle between good and evil and tip it all into the dumpster out back.

Emmy never lived to see my boys. She would have loved them. Interacting with them might have brought back some of the warmth and life to her that had slowly bled out over the decade or so she had left. She grew pale and skinny, with large, empty eyes and soft hair, soft movements, too quiet for anyone to make the effort to befriend. I loved her, but I knew she was only a lonely little wisp of a person, a faded afterglow of a presence somehow gone before she'd left the room. She made it to 16—the same age I was when she disappeared—before writing us a note, hiking out to the bridge that crosses the Wexton River, and jumping to her death very late one icy February night. She'd taken off her shoes—I never understood why suicide jumpers do that, but so many of them seem to—and placed them neatly next to an Ansel Adams book. The cops found her note tucked into the book, right at the page that was her favorite, the forest in the snow. The note simply read:

I need to find the beautiful places again.
Forgive me. I love you both. -E.

She was still looking to find that feeling again that the forest in the snow gave her. I like to think that wherever she is now—the last true great place where people who are missing in your life go—that she found it.

My father never sold the bookstore. I think part of him felt too responsible for it, and what it had been on the verge of becoming—what maybe, however dormant, it still was. He wouldn't have foisted that responsibility off on anyone else. He did come up to see me and his grandsons twice, and the boys loved him. He loved them too, but I could tell that any joy he took in spending time with them was undercut by a kind of tense fear. He worried to the point of panic when they were out of sight. He was hyper-vigilant with them, and it exhausted him. My father looked old before he was, and died alone of a brain aneurism in that same house, in that same chair, watching that same television that had made up so much of his life after Emmy disappeared. I cried a lot when he died, and it might make me sound like a bad daughter, but not all those tears were formed in sadness. Some were simply tears of relief. My father, God rest him, would never have to worry again.

One thing I can say is that I did grow up and marry my soul mate, and I did have two beautiful boys. I moved far away from my father's bookstore and we spent our summer vacations at the Delaware Water Gap instead of watching my father fall apart. I love my family, but lately I can see in my husband's eyes a kind of worried question he isn't quite ready to ask. I sense that he feels I'm slipping away from him. Shutting him out. Maybe I am; Lord knows I don't mean to, but I can't bear the thought that the things that haunted my sister and then my father, the things I think are taking a deeper hold in me, might poison him too. My boys look at me nowadays like I so often looked at my father. It makes me turn away from them sometimes, and I feel guilty for that. They may never realize that I'm only trying to protect them. I love them all so, so much, but if they look at me, and I mean, really look at me, they'll know.

I'm sure of that. It will be obvious in every part of me, in every way that the people who love you know. I don't want anything to strip the beauty out of life for them. I can't imagine imparting anything worse to the man and boys I love than despair.

Because I don't plan to let anyone read this, and in fact intend to burn it, I guess I can admit that the thought of putting them all out of this life has crossed my mind. More often lately, as I've been writing all this down. There are pills that would make it painless. They would all just fall asleep, and me with them, and then we wouldn't have to be there when the exodus of those things comes through...

I haven't worked up the guts to do it, though. Like I said, I love them. I am wife and mother, and those are protector roles. I want them to be safe. I can't keep them safe once they've gone beyond this world, nor can I quite believe wholeheartedly and without any doubt that there is someplace safe for them to go after death. I like to think there is—some days, absolutely need to believe it—but I don't really know.

What I am sure of is that there are many other rifts between worlds, not just the one behind the Arts & Photography bookcase in my father's used bookstore. I think we pass through them all the time. For example, sometimes you're driving, and you sort of zone out, and your thoughts, if asked to recall them later, weren't anything, really, just the daily drone of mental minutiae. But then you think all of a sudden that you ought to be paying more attention to the road because the turn is coming up, or the exit. And that's when you realize you're somehow many miles into your trip, that you've already made that turn or taken that exit and then some, and you can't remember doing any of it. I honestly believe some of those are soon-to-be-rifts, little spots weakening over time. I don't know if we're doing something to are, but the weave in that fabric of reality is wearing thin, and I don't think there's any force in anyone's universe with the capability to sew a patch over it.

And I have reason to believe that many of those spots all over the world have already torn open. I think the pressure behind them must be unbearable. I'm not just talking about the Stonehenges and Bermuda Triangles and the old pow-wow cursed land and the Native American exile grounds, but the Walmart parking lots and the cell phone dead zones on the New Jersey Turnpike and those heavy, ozone-smelling patches of fallow farmland where nothing (or nothing wholesome) seems to grow. All those little parts of safe, suburban America that we shiver in delight at talking about around campfires or on car rides. Places where folks could quite innocently wander right out of existence as we know it.

And folks have been.

See, the new statistics are out. The missing persons statistics for 2011, I mean. Incidents of people gone missing—men, women, children, the elderly—without a trace have tripled, not just since the 2001 stats, but since 2010. Since last year alone. And although I have a pretty good idea of where a number of those people have gone, I don't expect them to come back like Emmy did. She was a fluke, and although she physically returned to this side of the rift, she never really made it back.

It's not just the stats though, that make me think more rifts are opening all over the world. We have the internet now, and I can do all kinds of searches on statistics and related topics…even if they might not be recognized as related topics by anyone else. There are even message boards, blogs, and missing persons websites dedicated to disseminating information. Missing persons websites dedicated to

disseminating information, even. And when you sift through all that stuff and
piece it together, you start to get a pretty disturbing picture, more Escher than Adams. A picture that shows that if we can wander right through those rifts into other worlds, just like Emmy did, that other things, unspeakable, nasty, hateful things, can just as easily slip, plop, slither, crawl, or simply wander out.

Take, for example, the information I found on one George Colbert's missing persons web page. Colbert, 46, designer and copywriter for a small ad agency in Maryland, left his office one February night around 9:30 after calling his wife, Greta, to say he'd be home in the next fifteen minutes or so. His home in Columbia was about a ten- to fifteen-minute drive from his Baltimore office. Around 11 p.m., after making several unanswered calls to his cell and his office phone, his wife called the police. It sounds, from the web page, that the police were not immediately going to search for him—at least, not until it was relayed back to the station that around the same time Greta Colbert was speaking with the police, a patrolman found George's car off in a ditch on the side of the road. Two things struck police, family, and friends alike as exceedingly odd. The first was that the roadside ditch where George's car was found was about 155 miles away from Baltimore, and yet George's co-workers could place him in his office as late as 9 p.m. Even with two hours' drive time, how had he gotten so far from work or home, and why? The second—and here's the real kicker—was that only half his car was found. The passenger half. The car had been split lengthways down the middle, and both George and the half of the car in which he'd been sitting were just gone.

I've seen forces that can split things neatly like that, when in a state of flux. I think it's obvious where I'm going with this.

Or take as another example a poster on a message board who happened to casually mention the strange disappearance of acquaintance and fellow bar patron Dave Kohlar, 34, of Lakehaven, New Jersey, who apparently vanished into a late summer night in 2008. About sixteen or seventeen posts down, there is a simple anonymous comment: The Hollowers took him back through the rift. It goes unacknowledged by the thirty or so subsequent posters, but it's there. It's there, for people who are looking.

I found some really crazy things about this one apartment building up in New England that people are building on the site of what used to be an old asylum. There was apparently some kind of massacre there and the people of that town tore the asylum down. The land still being good, they've been trying to erect a very modern apartment building. The photos online of the old asylum could set a mind thinking as it is. And I don't discount the numerous warnings and complaints in the comment section of the historical society's webpage on the place— especially one commenter's seemingly unrelated rant about wounds in the earth swallowing up any health or sanity on that ground, and monsters shaping the darkness around the skeletal frame of the new building.

*

I've just reread this whole account and I think it covers everything I wanted or needed to say. It's very late and I'm tired now. My hands ache from grinding all those pills with a fork and my head aches. This afternoon, before I logged onto my laptop to finish this, I drove past my dad's old bookstore, and I swear I could smell that thick ozone smell of the rift, infesting the whole place. I could smell it all the way out on the street, in my car with the windows rolled up. And just before, I thought I saw something out the open bedroom window, something out on the lawn down there
that pulled and pushed the darkness like clay into shapes. That ozone smell was strong, coming from the front of the house. Whatever it was, it ran and hid when it saw me looking.

The house is too quiet tonight and this ache in my hands is spreading up to and out from my chest. My limbs feel so heavy and I'm so, so tired.

They're all safe now—my dad, my little Emmy, my boys, my dear Jason. But it still feels a lot like they're missing. And I just want to be with them.

Tomorrow I'll print this out and burn it all. So much work, just to burn it, but if it takes the bad away and sets the world right for even just a little while, even just until the pills I've crushed for myself can take hold, then it's worth it. I hope the things from beyond the rift choke on the smoke of it.

I want to find the beautiful places, too. hope there are some, on the other side of death. One last

rift to cross through.
　　I am so tired.

*

*NOTES OF FIRE CHIEF JOE GIBBONS to
HAMMOND HOUSE FIRE FILE*

*Microsoft Word document (file name ForEmmy.doc)
found on personal laptop of
one Dana Marie (McCluskey) Hammond, June 11th,
2011 – suicide note?*

*Hammond family members positioned on front porch
with laptop, far opposite the site of the fire's point of
origin.*

*Mr. Jason Hammond (35), found deceased—
suppressed respiratory system due to overdose of
sedatives, combined with smoke inhalation. Two sons,
David (6) and Gregory (4) hospitalized for lung
damage from smoke and for sedative overdoses.
Children remain comatose as of this notation to case
file.*

*As of this writing, the whereabouts of Dana
Hammond remain unknown.*

CPSIA information can be obtained
at www.ICGtesting.com
Printed in the USA
LVHW09s2154260818
588184LV00001B/10/P

9 781492 708094